Letters to Leo

Amy Hest

Letters TO LEO

illustrated by Julia Denos

CANDLEWICK PRESS

Text copyright © 2012 by Amy Hest
Illustrations copyright © 2012 by Julia Denos

First edition 2012

Library of Congress Cataloging-in-Publication Data is available.

Library of Congress Catalog Card Number 2011045901

ISBN 978-0-7636-3695-1

12 13 14 15 16 17 BVG 10 9 8 7 6 5 4 3 2 1

Printed in Berryville, VA, U.S.A.

This book was typeset in Humana Sans.
The illustrations were done in mixed media.

Candlewick Press
99 Dover Street
Somerville, Massachusetts 02144

visit us at www.candlewick.com

For Lon, for-ever
A. H.

To all the stories that live in Riverside Park
J. D.

Model Citizen LEO.

November 13

Dear Leo,

Welcome to apartment 10B! Welcome to your new home! You are now an official member of the Rossi family . . . and guess what? You are the first ever Rossi DOG. So, congratulations. You made it.

We weren't going to get a dog. Ever. Because of my father. All my life, I kept saying, I WANT A DOG! I WANT A DOG! But no dog. Because of my father.

HE DOES NOT LOVE DOGS.

I finally figured out why he doesn't love dogs. It has to do with being brave. See, some fathers are BIG and BRAVE. My father is TALL, but he isn't that brave. Sometimes he pretends to be. But *I* know the truth. *I* know he is secretly afraid of things. All kinds of things. Such as bugs and tall ladders and the ocean when the waves are too high. And large dogs.

HE MIGHT EVEN BE AFRAID OF **ALL** DOGS.
EVEN LITTLE CUTIES LIKE **YOU**.

That's why you have to be a good boy, Leo. A nice,
little perfect Rossi, okay? Chin up, baby! It's not that
hard! Just do everything I say every single day, and
presto change-o . . . my father isn't afraid of dogs
anymore! We all live happily ever after.

~~Very truly yours,~~
~~Yours very truly,~~
~~Your truest friend,~~
Love you, Leo!
Annie

*Also. I made you a merry little workbook. WE
SHALL READ YOUR WORKBOOK EVERY DAY.
Try, try, try. It's important to try hard.

LEO'S WORKBOOK

HOW TO BE A GOOD DOG
AND PERFECT LITTLE ROSSI

1. Wag a lot. Be cheerful, not grumpy.
2. Pretend my father is your best friend, even though your best friend is ME.
3. Be a good eater and don't waste food and don't make faces if you don't like the food.
4. Watch baseball on TV with my father. Root for the Yankees. It's important.
5. Be polite to all the neighbors, and no jumping on the neighbors.
6. No loud barking in apartment 10B. *In case of EMERGENCY (such as a big bad robber in the house), you may bark a lot. You may BITE the robber.

This is the longest letter I ever wrote and my hand is falling off! But don't worry, Leo, I promise to write you more great letters. <u>Short</u> ones, ha! With lots of secrets, ha! And I will read you all my letters late at night and nobody knows. Just you! Just me!

November 15

Dear Leo,

Well, of *course* I'm not supposed to do things that are sneaky . . . but too bad.

> I *love* sneaking you in my bed!
> And *yo ho ho*!
> My father doesn't know!

Poor Leo, you were cold on the cold floor. You were lonely in the lonely night. *Someone* had to save you. So I put you in my bed . . . and saved you.

LEO'S LULLABY

Good night, Leo!
Sleep tight, Leo!
Don't snore, Leo!
And don't get caught!

Signed,
Miss Sneaky

November 16

Dear Leo,

Don't be sad, okay? And don't blame me. Because
it's not my fault. Sure, I want to stay home with you,
but I *have* go to school tomorrow. All kids do. It's
the LAW and my father won't let me break the LAW.
Ever. Which is a big shame. Because fourth grade is
a lot of *hard work*. Especially if your teacher is Mrs.
No-Fun Bailey. In room 245 you have to be serious
at all times. And *follow directions* at all times, etc. If
you're 100% *perfect* at all times, then you're a *model
citizen*, and Mrs. B puts your name on the bulletin
board, and your picture, and a story about *you* and
all your good deeds, etc. Last week, Pauline was
model citizen. That's her second time this year, so
let's not like Pauline, ha!

You know who's lucky? Third graders. Especially
if your teacher is Miss Meadows. Sometimes after
school I go back to third grade again, to room 107
and Miss Meadows all over again. I always say, HI,
MISS MEADOWS! And she always says, WELCOME

BACK TO ROOM 107, ANNIE! I look around for a while. Then I go home, good-bye.

   Well, try not to miss me too much when I'm in school. Mrs. Peterman promised to take you for walks. She's good at taking care of me (when my father's at work), but she doesn't know too much about how to walk my little dog. So <u>behave</u> yourself.

Love,
Annie

I know!
Just look at
my picture
all day.
Then you'll
be happy,
not sad!

November 20

Dear Leo,

You probably don't care about poetry. Neither do I.
Mrs. Bailey cares, and now we have to be gifted
fourth-grade poets. WE ARE *ALL* GIFTED POETS,
BOYS AND GIRLS . . . *Blaaahhh!* Today she made us
write *a short poem with a dash of humor.* I tried and
tried. Nothing. I went up to Mrs. B and whispered,
I CAN'T WRITE A POEM, MRS. B. She wasn't that
nice. GO BACK TO YOUR SEAT, ANNIE. . . . KEEP
TRYING, ANNIE. . . . CLOSE YOUR EYES AND
PICTURE SOMETHING YOU LIKE, ANNIE. I was
mad. I pictured things I *don't* like: (1) Mrs. Bailey,
(2) poetry, (3) dividing fractions, (4) Reptiles.

Still no poem. Still mad. Then a picture of a
great big *cupcake* popped into my head! *Mmnnn,
cupcakes!!* Then I wrote *a short poem with a dash
of humor.* Even the title is funny! "Cupcakes in the
Rain." But here comes the *sad* part of the story.
Nobody laughed when I read it out loud. Not even
Mrs. Bailey. Not even Jean-Marie, my so-called best
friend in my class. Then Edward Noble read his

stupid poem, "The Goldfish Ate My Homework," and *everyone* laughed and Mrs. B said, WHY, EDWARD, WHAT A CHARMING, FUNNY POEM! Which it was NOT.

I threw my poem in the garbage after school, but now I want it back to show my father. He always loves everything I write.

Show-off + Bad Poet = Edward Noble

No more poetry.

Annie

November 26

Dear Leo,

We have a little problem, my friend. It has to do with your elevator manners. Which aren't that great.

You may not bark at people in the elevator.

Why? Because it's RUDE and you scared that little boy Sam who lives in 3C. You made him cry, Leo. The neighbors won't like us anymore if you're bad. You want cookie-treats, right? Then be GOOD and follow the rules.

Your true,
Annie

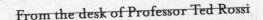

You know what I love? Writing
secret letters (to you) in my bed
late at night . . . and my father
thinks I'm sleeping, but I'm not,
and you snuggle up close. Also I
love reading (to you) in my soft
night voice . . . and you are a
good but sleepy listener. A long
time ago before she died, my mother
read to me in her soft night voice
and I curled up close, just like
you, and sometimes I fell asleep,
just like you.

December 2

Dear Leo,

Do you think I squint a lot? Because my father
said the same exact thing three days in a row.
Monday! Tuesday! Wednesday! WHAT'S UP WITH
THE SQUINTING, ANNIE? WHAT'S UP WITH THE
SQUINTING, ANNIE? I WONDER IF YOU NEED
GLASSES, ANNIE. Worry, worry. That's all he loves to
do is *worry*. I *don't* squint, and I *don't* want glasses.
Exception: sunglasses. The bigger the better, and
you may not believe this, but I look *sensational*
and *gorgeous* in sunglasses, ha! *Here she comes! It's
Annie "the movie star" Rossi!*

Don't squint, Leo.
Annie

Important Subject:
Cooperation and Showing off.

No offense, but you forgot to show off in
front of Jean-Marie, the way we practiced.
Such as when I said, SIT, LEO, you forgot
to sit. When I said, PAW, LEO, you forgot
to give me your paw. It's embarrassing.
Plus, you smiled too much at Jean-Marie,
and you forgot to smile at me. I forgive
you. But in the future, you have to
cooperate and show off when there's a guest
in the house. Then
everyone knows what a
good dog trainer I am.

A

December 14

Dear Leo,

Remember that picture that I took? The one of you barking at my father in the park? I showed it to Miss Meadows after school. She liked it so much! She said, WHAT A COUPLE OF CHARACTERS! Then I was looking around at all the usual stuff on her desk. Such as two blue pens . . . five pencils . . . one Daily Lesson Planner . . . third-grade spelling tests in a pile . . . third-grade book reports in a pile, etc. Then I saw something unusual — a tall yellow birthday card, and her name was on the card!

Me: IS IT YOUR *BIRTHDAY*, MISS MEADOWS?

Miss Meadows: YES, ANNIE, AND I CAN'T BELIEVE I'M *32!*

Me: AT LEAST YOU'RE NOT AS OLD AS MY FATHER. *HE'S* ALMOST *40.* HAPPY BIRTHDAY, MISS MEADOWS!

Then I went home.

Your favorite character,

Me

P.S. I wish I made Miss M. a beautiful birthday card, but I didn't. Okay, next year on her birthday I will make her one. Remind me, Leo.

December 17

Dear Leo,

You want my father to like you, right?

THEN BE A <u>MODEL</u> <u>CITIZEN</u> AND STOP STEALING HIS SLIPPERS EVERY NIGHT.

See, *I* think you're the most hilarious dog in the world, and I love chasing you around the house, yelling, STOP THAT THIEF! CATCH THAT THIEF! The problem as usual is Mr. Grumpy. He does *not* find you hilarious. I'M <u>NOT</u> AMUSED, LEO. . . . THIS IS <u>NOT</u> A GAME, LEO. . . . HAND OVER THE SLIPPERS, LEO. . . . BAD DOG, LEO. . . .

You're not a bad dog. You're just having a little fun, right? Kids like me, and dogs like you, we're good at being funny. We're good at having fun. Grown-ups only care about *boring* things. Such as *ed-u-ca-tion*. Being *po-lite*. Not riding your bike *too fast*, etc.

BORING. BORING. BORING.

I'm glad I'm not a grown-up.

Annie

Why do you love those slippers so much anyway? They're old. *Yucky*. They look like *mashed potatoes*.

December 18

Dear Leo,

Finally! It finally happened! We *learned* something in fourth grade. It's about <u>juicy</u> words, and I shall now tell you all about <u>juicy</u> words. They're more <u>exciting</u> than regular words. They <u>describe</u>. Mrs. Bailey says, INTERESTING WRITERS CHOOSE JUICY WORDS, BOYS AND GIRLS. For homework we have to write a <u>pretend</u> letter (to someone NOT in your family) with eight (or more) <u>juicy</u> words. I wrote one to Miss Meadows. It's about YOU. I already told her all about you, but it's a <u>pretend</u> letter. Meaning I don't have to mail it. But I might.

Dear Miss Meadows,

Hi! It's Annie Rossi! How are you? I am fine, thank you.

The Rossi family got a dog! He came with a name. Which is Leo. He is <u>smart</u> and <u>funny</u> and <u>handsome</u>.

His color is <u>tan</u>. He has a <u>scraggly</u> beard. His <u>shiny</u> tag says, MY NAME IS LEO ROSSI. IF LOST, PLEASE RETURN ME TO 440 RIVERSIDE DRIVE, NYC. Leo sleeps in my room. He loves my <u>cozy</u> bed, but my father makes up a lot of <u>boring</u> rules. Such as (1) A DOG IN THE BED IS NOT A GOOD SLEEPING ARRANGEMENT, LEO; (2) NO DOGS ON THE COUCH, LEO.

Sometimes my father falls asleep in his work clothes on the couch. Then sneaky Leo sneaks right up! Now they're BOTH sleeping on the couch. . . . *Shhhh!!*

Your fourth grader,
Annie R.

Leo Diagram

Scraggly

Shiny

Also: smart (Leo)
funny (Leo♥)
handsome (Leo)
cozy (my bed)
boring (rules!)

January 4

Dear Leo,

Well? Notice anything different about my face?
Because something's different, definitely. It's still
me . . . but . . . it's me in brown glasses. First I *loved* them
(in the eyeglass store). Then I *hated* them (on the way
home). Now I *love* them again. Maybe. A little. I can't
decide. I'm only allowed to wear them for reading,
that's it. My father says a lot of his college kids wear
brown glasses. And also *Miss America*.

Your Miss America,
Annie

January 7

Dear Leo,

All right, buddy-boy, the party's over. It's time to *shape up*. Why? Because my father is FED UP. Do you know what that means? It means he's FED UP. With YOU. Not ALL of you. Just the PART of you that wants to have a PARTY at *5 o'clock in the morning*. I figured out why he is FED UP. It has to do with PERSONALITY. See, *some* people (such as me) are always cheerful, because we have a *cheerful* personality. Even when my dog wakes me up at 5:00 a.m. *Other* people (such as my father) have a *serious* personality, and sometimes worse. Meaning a *grumpy* personality. Especially when a *certain little dog* (such as you) pulls the blanket off his bed and *licks his toes* to say good morning.

I shall now tell you how to *shape up* in the morning. Pay attention to Annie's Mighty Fine Morning Rules.

ANNIE'S MIGHTY FINE MORNING RULES

1.   <u>BE QUIET</u> at 5:00 a.m. No barking hello. No loud sniffing and snorting. No pulling off blankets. No licking toes, noses, etc.

2.   You're allowed to wake me up at <u>6:30 a.m.</u>

3.   Then (together) we tell my father, "Wake up! Wake up! It's time to walk Leo!"

4.   Then (together) *The Rossi Family Goes Out For A Walk* and no one is FED UP, hurrah!

Party, party, party!
Annie

January 8

Dear Leo,

Not a good day at PS 88.

1 CATASTROPHE #1 (FRACTIONS): Mrs. B gave

back our math tests about dividing fractions and I
was hoping for 100%. No luck. There only were four
(teeny-tiny) mistakes! But Mrs. B-for-bad Bailey
wrote ANNIE, PLEA SE SEE ME across the top of my test.
That's INSULTING, Mrs. B! So now I have to get
extra help in math. After school on Monday. Also
INSULTING.

2 CATASTROPHE #2 (ART): Mrs. Pasternak

forgot to say my new painting was *quite compelling*,
which is what she always says about *Pauline's* stuff
in art, and Matt's stuff in art. My painting *is* quite
compelling. It's a picture of YOU and ME in the
library, and we are reading a book about dogs. Right
there in the library.

3 **CATASTROPHE #3 (SPELLING BEE):** Well that's my very *best* thing in fourth grade and all week long I can't wait to be a spelling star but Edward Noble won the spelling bee today (all because of "vivacious") so now everyone thinks he's a better speller than me. Which he is NOT.

4 **CATASTROPHE #4 (CHATTER):** It was 2:45 p.m. Almost the weekend! Finally! Mrs. B said, BOYS AND GIRLS, THERE IS TOO MUCH <u>CHATTER</u> IN THIS ROOM . . . and she was looking right at *me* when she said it. Even though the whole entire class was CHATTERING.

I hope *you* never have four catastrophes.

Annie

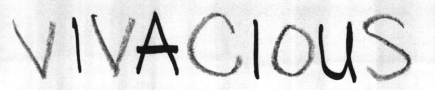

VIVACIOUS

January 11

Dear Leo,

It wouldn't KILL them. To let you come in for one little minute on a rainy afternoon. You were frozen. Shivering. Plus, I wanted to show you to Miss Madison, my favorite librarian. You know what? I USED to like libraries and librarians, but not anymore. All they care about is RULES. *No eating in the library. . . . No drinking in the library. . . . No loud talking in the library. . . . No dancing in the library. . . . No dogs in the library.*

If they won't let my dog in the library, then good-bye library. I'm never going back. Miss Madison will be sorry. She'll be crying. WE NEED <u>ANNIE</u> —DEAR, CHEERFUL <u>ANNIE</u> —IN THE LIBRARY! Okay, *fine.* I'll go back. Maybe. I need to return my book from last week. And get some more. But I'm still pretty mad. M-A-D. And if I made the rules, Rule #1 is called BRING YOUR DOG TO THE LIBRARY.

WISH, WISH! I wish you would fit in my pocket!
Then I could sneak you into the library! And
everywhere else!

Your library girl,
Annie

Pocket
Leo!!
(sooooo CUTE)

Sneaky
Sneaky LEO

January 16

Dear Leo,

I know who ate the sandwich. My father's chicken sandwich.

CLUE #1: BREAD IN YOUR BEARD

CLUE #2: MAYONNAISE IN YOUR BEARD

I'm surprised he isn't even mad at you. He just wants to have a little man-to-man *talk* with you. About taking food off his desk, etc. He's looking everywhere for you! ALL IS FORGIVEN, LEO. . . . YOU CAN STOP HIDING NOW, LEO. . . . But he forgets to look under my bed! Don't worry, I'll never tell where you are. Or what you did. Best friends are NOT tattletales.

Your best,
Annie

January 21

Dear Leo,

I have a job! A REAL job, in school. You get a
BADGE. You walk down the hall and everyone sees
your badge.

I AM A READING BUDDY.

Reading buddies *help*. You have to be in fourth
grade like me and then you get your very own first
grader and I got Charley. First you go to room 100 at
11:15. You find Charley. Then you practice reading.
You have to be responsible. And serious. And kind.
You are the teacher.

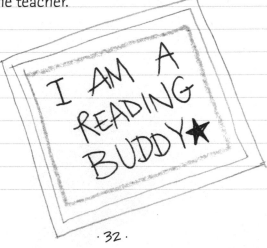

DON'T WORRY. SOON YOU'LL BE A GOOD
READER LIKE ME. That's what I tell Charley. We
have a special blue folder. I hope he likes me!

If I had a little brother, I wish it could be Charley.

Love,

the great reading buddy

P.S. Miss Meadows says I look slightly *mysterious*
(in my glasses). And *terribly* wise. I agree with Miss
Meadows. She knows a lot. Plus, she's pretty.

January 26

SUBJECT: WHY IN THE WORLD DOES MY FATHER GO TO A DINNER PARTY WITHOUT ME?

I do NOT approve! He's SUPPOSED to be having dinner HERE. With US, Leo. At six as usual. In our very own kitchen. Plus, Tuesday is hamburger-and-baked-potato night, and he's supposed to be cooking hamburgers and I toast buns, set table, etc. Now Mrs. Peterman is doing everything and I'm not in the mood to be a good helper. Too bad. I'm surprised she's taking *his* side not mine. YOUR FATHER IS VERY DEVOTED TO YOU, ANNIE. . . . IT'S GOOD FOR HIM TO SPEND AN EVENING NOW AND THEN WITH GROWN-UPS. . . . Wrong, wrong, wrong! He doesn't even *like* dinner parties. He *told* me! TO BE HONEST, ANNIE, I DON'T EVEN *LIKE* DINNER PARTIES. . . . I'M NOT EXACTLY A **SOCIAL BUTTERFLY** THESE DAYS. . . .

It's not fair. Nobody ever takes me to a dinner party.

Your social butterfly,

Annie

At least he wore the *red* tie, the one I
like, with monkeys, and not that boring blue
one. My mother used to sit on the bed and
talk about things when he was tying his tie.
Once he kissed her on the nose, right on
the tip of it, right in the middle of tying
his tie, and I said NO MORE KISSING and it
wasn't supposed to be a joke but everyone
laughed anyway.

January 29

Dear Leo,

Some people have all the luck. Such as Jean-Marie.
She eats cookies during math time and never gets
caught. But when I put one teeny cookie in my
mouth during math time, Mrs. B gives me a look
that means I'M SURPRISED AT YOU, ANNIE. So now
I feel like a big fat criminal. Which I am not. Jean-
Marie is Mrs. Bailey's favorite. Plus, she's a math
genius. Which I am not. I wish I could be perfect.
Like Jean-Marie.

Your not criminal,

Annie

P.S. You stay here, Leo. I'm going to the kitchen. *Shhhh!*
To get 2 cookies — One for you. One for me. *Shhhh!*
Don't be a tattletale.

February 1

Dear Leo,

Will you kindly stop sulking! I'm *sorry*, okay? I'm sorry I said, WHY CAN'T YOU BE LIKE THAT DOG, LEO? . . . And I ~~promise swear~~ solemnly swear I like you more. It's just that he did everything that lady told him to do. Such as when she said, GET THE BALL, MASON . . . Mason got the ball *and* brought it back *and* dropped it at her feet. Which is pretty smart. Also he wasn't a maniac in the park chasing squirrels like some dogs I know.

Okay, I shall now tell you my favorite part about having a dog. It's *walking* you. Early in the morning. Before breakfast. Before school. Before the city wakes up. And we're the only ones up. You, me, my father, and the *moon*. I never knew about the moon in the morning before I had a dog.

Your true admirer,

Annie

February 4

Dear Leo,

At least you don't smell anymore, but next time
you get a bath, I'm wearing a <u>bathing suit</u>, not my
regular clothes. Your bath is *hard work,* pal, and
you get a big fat zero for *cooperation.* Flooding the
bathroom floor = NOT cooperation. Plus, I hate
that yucky mop; it's not fair *I* had to mop. Oh well, I
forgive you as usual.

Your soaking wet,

Annie

You love when I take your picture, don't you, Mr.
Funny? You just look at the camera and wag. Ha, ha,
funny, funny!

February 8

Dear Leo,

Mrs. B says, WE ALL HAVE A STORY TO TELL, BOYS
AND GIRLS. She's wrong. Because I have about a
million stories to tell. That's why I should maybe
write some books. I could write one about you, *Leo!*

YOU AND YOUR DOG: TIPS FOR GETTING ALONG AND HAVING FUN!
by Annie Rossi

I know — another book with *tips* in the title. *YOU
AND YOUR ELDERLY PARENT: TIPS FOR GETTING
ALONG AND HAVING FUN,* by Dr. Silvio Silverman.
I saw it. In the library. In the Adult Reading Room.
The Adult Reading Room is a very boring place,
with about a million boring books. But this one had
a shiny red cover, and red is my favorite color, so I
peeked inside. I found a good tip on page 32.

TIP #3: ENCOURAGE YOUR ELDERLY PARENT TO TRY NEW THINGS.

I figured out something BIG. *I have an elderly parent (my father) and he *always* does the same old thing, yikes! Such as when we go to the library. He takes too long picking books. Always! Such as in the park. He sits on the same old bench and *reads*. Always! Poor sweet Daddy. I SHALL ENCOURAGE HIM TO TRY NEW THINGS! Thank you, Dr. Silvio Silverman!

DAD # **1** (boring)

NOTE

To: Daddy
From: Annie
Subject: Father Darling,
You Should Try New Things!

1. You always put blueberry jam on your toast. A lot of people like blackberries. Try blackberry jam. You'll be happy.
2. You always sit on a bench in the park. Try something new! Such as a handstand in the park! You'll be happy.

DAD #2 (cool)

February 10

Dear Leo,

Now guess what happened? It's about Jean-Marie.
She got a little famous today, due to she fell out of
a tree and broke her right arm and now there's a
beautiful cast on her arm. Which everyone signed,
and she chose *me* to sign first (because she likes
me best). I wrote: BETTER GET BETTER FAST! LOVE, ANNIE
AND LEO. Then it was lunchtime. In honor of her
broken arm, I said, YOU CAN HAVE MY CUPCAKE,
JEAN-MARIE. Well, I never knew she would eat the
WHOLE THING. But that's what she did. And now
there was nothing for me, *not even one crumb.* Then
she turned into this big drama queen. She held her
poor little broken arm in the air and sighed a poor
little broken arm sigh and said, BEST FRIENDS LIKE
US SHARE *EVERYTHING* (Sigh, sigh. Drama, drama).
WE SHOULD **SHARE** LEO . . . AND THEN MY ARM
FEELS BETTER RIGHT AWAY! ALL BECAUSE OF LEO.

Well she's crazy, because I'm *never* sharing you! Never! Never! Never! Not even if she has two broken arms! C-R-A-Z-Y. That girl just *loves* to copy me. Such as last year when I got red sneakers, then *she* got red sneakers. Now I have a dog, so *she* wants a dog. I wouldn't mind a broken arm too much. Everyone wants to sign your cast . . . carry your lunch tray . . . sit next to you . . . etc. Break your arm and presto change-o . . . you are popular.

Love,
Miss Not-Too-Popular

ean-Marie   v.s.   Me (Annie)

(copy)   (original)

February 15

Dear Leo,

I know you like to chew stuff, but you may *not* chew that umbrella. I mean it. I'm serious. I mean it. Chew a bone. Chew a sock. Chew bacon. But not the yellow umbrella. See, it reminds me of rainy days . . . and rainy days remind me of my mother. Because she liked and loved a rainy day. A lot of people (such as my father) get mad at the weatherman whenever he says, YOU'LL BE NEEDING THAT UMBRELLA TODAY, FOLKS! Not me. Not you. *We* get happy in the rain, don't we, Leo? A lot of dogs hate going out in the rain. They just stand around looking miserable and wet. Not you, baby. You *bounce* off the stoop! Just like me. Just like my mother in the rain.

Love you,
Annie

February 17

Dear Leo,

Stupid, stupid Edward. *He* started, not me. *He* was mean, not me. All because I'm terrible in volleyball. Especially *serving,* and I was *trying* so hard to serve *over* the net. And then Edward said something mean in his mean little voice: "And now Bossy Annie Rossi will serve into the net, as usual!" I was so mad and so furious. But then a miracle happened at Public School 88.

I HIT IT <u>OVER</u> THE NET!

I was so happy! I was even laughing! In gym! Then <u>trouble</u>. Edward was yelling and holding his nose. SHE BROKE MY NOSE! SHE BROKE MY NOSE! ANNIE ROSSI BROKE MY NOSE! Then Miss Mahoney (mean gym teacher) said, WHY, ANNIE ROSSI! WE DO <u>NOT</u> LAUGH WHEN SOMEONE IS HURT! YOU CAN MARCH YOURSELF DOWN TO THE PRINCIPAL'S OFFICE AT ONCE!

I was SO SCARED. Plus, my feelings were hurt. Plus, I *hated* Miss Mahoney. Even though it's not nice to hate.

At first, Mr. Levine was on the phone. I sat on the couch in his office. (I never knew a principal has a red couch. And a jar of cookies on his desk.) Then he was off the phone. HELLO THERE, ANNIE. HOW ABOUT A COOKIE? . . . THEN WE'LL TALK. I wasn't too hungry, but the cookies looked good so I had one. Then I told him the story about how I *finally* got the ball over the net and how I *wasn't* aiming for Edward's nose. I'm not that kind of girl! I started to cry. Mr. Levine gave me a tissue. He didn't yell. Or even act mad. He told me something. If someone such as Edward is mean or teasing you, *ignore* him. It's hard, but you can do it. I have to write two Letters of Apology.

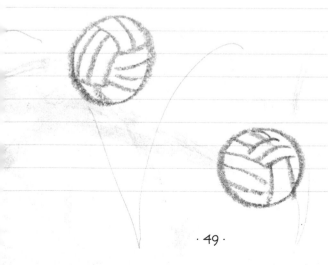

LETTER OF APOLOGY #1: TO MISS MAHONEY

LETTER OF APOLOGY #2: TO EDWARD

Then the school nurse came in to say Edward's nose is BRUISED, not BROKEN. Then it was lunchtime and I went to the cafeteria and Edward had a blue ice pack on his nose. He ate a lot, so I guess his nose didn't hurt that much.

Now I'll never be a model citizen. Ever.
Your poor little,

Annie

February 23

Dear Leo,

Guess what? You'll never guess what! Mrs. Bailey, my teacher, is going to have a baby! I HAVE NICE NEWS, BOYS AND GIRLS. *BEAUTIFUL* NEWS. IN JUNE I AM HAVING A BABY. We cheered and clapped and made so much noise. Then it was, CALM DOWN, BOYS AND GIRLS. . . . IT'S TIME TO GO TO THE ART ROOM, BOYS AND GIRLS. . . . QUICKLY. . . . QUIETLY. . . . All day long I kept peeking at Mrs. B's stomach. So far it looks regular. I wish she could name the baby Annie. I can't wait to hold baby Annie!

Love,
Annie

I wish we had a baby in this house. She could sleep in my room, and if she cries at night, we hug her a lot and nobody's lonely in the middle of the night. Her name is Louise. *Aiiieeee!* I have an idea! Now pay attention to my great idea! First, we find someone. Someone *extremely* nice. She has to like kids. And dogs. And my father . . . and . . . THEN he MARRIES her. And THEN we get a baby! Then we get baby Louise! It's my best idea! Ever!

March 2

Dear Leo,

I'm *done.* Done being friends with Jean-Marie. So good-bye, Jean-Marie. Why? Because two days in a row I save her a seat at lunch and she pretends to forget we always save seats. She sits with Pauline and I have no one to sit with but *boys.*

A lot of girls don't like boys. I like *some* boys *sometimes,* such as that downstairs neighbor-boy Drew. He used to be unfriendly, due to he's a big-shot seventh-grader. But fifteen Fridays ago he got nice. That's the day he brought an *adorable* little dog upstairs to 10B. (Which was you, Leo.) Drew hugged little adorable you and said three things in a sad voice.

1. HIS NAME IS LEO.
2. HE'S TEN MONTHS OLD.
3. MY MOTHER WON'T LET ME KEEP HIM.

Cute cute
CUTE
baby
Leo

I said two things.

1. I'LL TAKE HIM.
2. PLEASE, DADDY, PLEASE, DADDY, PLEASE!

Then it was quiet in the doorway. My father was looking deep in your eyes. You looked deep in his eyes. Then he put a finger in the air and said seven magic words.

THE DOG IN THE DOORWAY CAN STAY.

And *that* is the story of how you got to be a Rossi. All because of a *boy*.

Hip, hip, hooray!
Annie

The DOG
in
the
DOORWAY
can
STAY!!!

·55·

March 6

I *tried* to save you, Leo, so don't blame me.

Before we left the house, I tried. (2:45 p.m.)

Me: LEO DOESN'T *NEED* A HAIRCUT! HE'S PERFECT JUST THE WAY HE IS!

My father: PERHAPS, ANNIE, BUT HE'LL BE EVEN *MORE* PERFECT <u>AFTER</u> HIS HAIRCUT.

I tried some more. In front of Dolly's Dog Grooming Salon. (3:00 p.m.)

Me: SEE THAT TAIL, DADDY? IT'S ALL THE WAY DOWN. MEANING LEO'S UNHAPPY. HE WANTS TO GO *HOME*.

My father: AIIIEEE! YOU'RE BREAKING MY *HEART*, LEO.

Then he carried you inside for your haircut. He was whispering secret man-to-man stuff in your left ear, but I heard anyway. YOU'LL GET THROUGH IT, BUDDY. WE ALL GET THROUGH STUFF, AND YOU WILL, TOO.

Then we went outside. For ice cream. To cheer ourselves up. I had a chocolate cone. My father ordered vanilla. Then changed his mind and copied me. Chocolate.

Leo (before haircut)

We walked around the block five times in a row (3:40 p.m.). Then one more time. Then we went back to Dolly's. (3:45 p.m.).

It was all over, and here comes Mr. Beautiful!
You! Your tail was up and you looked so cute!
Then my father took your picture, so that we
can always remember the day of your haircut.

Look at the camera, Leo! Smile!

Annie

March 8

Dear Leo,

I might win a contest! It's for young city authors and I am a young city author! For the contest you write an *inspiring* essay about your *great idea for a better New York*. The winner gets to meet the mayor of New York City! There's a party in your classroom and the mayor comes to your party! He shakes your hand! You are now the most famous child at Public School 88! You might be on TV! You get a trophy! I hope it's me! I never got a trophy before. I've been thinking and thinking about my *inspiring* essay, but no ideas. Mrs. B says, PUNCTUATION COUNTS, BOYS AND GIRLS. SPELLING COUNTS. WRITE CLEARLY. My father says, WRITE ABOUT THINGS CLOSE TO YOUR HEART, ANNIE.

Must win contest! Must win contest!

Your city author,

Annie

SUBJECT: SLEEPOVER. Jean-Marie's having one when the cast comes off. Well, *maybe.* If her parents say yes, and I HOPE they say yes! Let's pray that Pauline can't come. Pray, pray, pray!

March 10

Dear Leo,

Today Mr. Levine came to room 245 to make sure Mrs. Bailey is a good teacher. We all raised our hands a lot and pretended to love school, especially fourth grade. We didn't want Mrs. B to get in trouble with the principal. We were like a team. Team Bailey. I wish her baby would be born tomorrow instead of June and she brings her to school in a carriage. When I was a baby I weighed seven pounds and two ounces. My mother told me that. Plus, I have seen my birth certificate.

I know something. It's about Mr. Levine. He is married to Mrs. Levine! A long time ago when I was a little first grader, she was my teacher. She's SO nice and she taught me how to read. And that's how I got to be such a good reader. I never knew that a teacher likes to marry the principal!

Will you marry me, Leo? Ha, ha!

Annie

March 12

Dear Leo,

Well, this is bad. Because now I have to be partners
with Edward for a social studies report. B-A-D. It's
Mrs. B's idea. Which proves she doesn't like me. I
have to go to the library with Edward, but I'm not
sitting next to him. Forget that. He can sit wherever
he wants in the library as long as it's FAR AWAY
FROM ME. The report is about LIFE IN THE CITY:
THE MUSEUMS OF NEW YORK. Museums are *not*
my favorite place to go in New York. Exception: the
Museum of Natural History. I like the dinosaurs
there. And also the cafeteria.

I. AM. SO. SICK. AND. TIRED. OF. FOURTH. GRADE. AND. EDWARD.

Annie

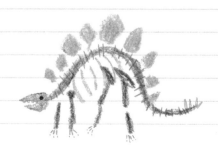

March 21

INTERESTING SUBJECT: SMELLY SOCKS. I caught you in the hamper again. Looking for my father's green socks again. To hide under the kitchen table again. You are *ridiculous*. Don't you know smelly socks *smell*?

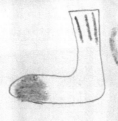

NOT INTERESTING SUBJECT: EDWARD IN THE LIBRARY. All he talks about is Henry, his *noble* GOLDFISH. Henry this and Henry that, and I don't know why he cares about a goldfish so much. He's always working on this teeny little comic book called *Henry Noble: The Adventures of a Noble Goldfish*. He does *that* in the library, and I get to do everything about MUSEUMS. He's lucky I'm not a tattletaling kind of person, or I would say to Mrs. B, SOMEONE'S DOING N-O-T-H-I-N-G AT THE LIBRARY.

SUBJECT: THE MEAN THING I ONCE SAID TO MY FATHER AND THIS IS WEIRD. IT'S ABOUT A GOLDFISH.

It was before we had a dog and I only wanted a dog and one day he said (in a really happy voice), YOU KNOW WHAT THIS FAMILY NEEDS, ANNIE? A *GOLDFISH*! HOW ABOUT GOING TO THE PET SHOP AND YOU CAN PICK OUT YOUR VERY OWN GOLDFISH! Well, that was the *worst* idea he ever had. *Ever.* I wasn't that nice. Me: A GOLDFISH IS NOT A PUPPY! That's what I said. I said it *loud* and *mean*. I hurt his feelings. I wish I never said it. I'm horrible.

Henry Noble:

the adventures of a
Noble
Goldfish.

March 23

Dear Leo,

Do you think I'll win that contest about a better New York? I really want that trophy, and I'll put it on the table next to my bed. Next to the picture of my mother. That's the best place for a trophy. I worked so hard on my essay and I *have* to win. Oh well, probably I won't win. Just like I won't ever be a model citizen in room 245. I've never won anything. Okay, one exception: spelling bees. So far I won seven of those in fourth grade! Okay, I shall now read my essay to you. Pay attention, please! It's important.

SPELLING BEES
x7

A BETTER NEW YORK:
My Inspiring Essay
By Annie Rossi, Fourth Grade

My name is Annie Rossi and I live in New
York City and I have a great idea for a
better New York. It's about dogs. A lot of
people such as me like and love dogs. The
problem is all those terrible signs. They
all say the same terrible thing. Which is:

NO DOGS ALLOWED!

1. PUBLIC LIBRARY. NO DOGS ALLOWED! My
   father loves books and the library and
   taking me to the library. My dog, Leo,
   loves walking with us to the library.
   Even if it's raining. You know what's
   sad? When Leo has to wait outside in the
   rain. (Because of the terrible sign.)
   It breaks your HEART. A lot of kids
   don't like libraries. (Too quiet, etc.)
   They need a new sign. It says, WE LOVE
   DOGS. BRING YOUR DOG TO THE LIBRARY! Now kids

love the library! They read one hundred
books! Grown-ups are finally happy.

2. PUBLIC SCHOOL 88. NO DOGS ALLOWED! I go
   to school every day. I don't mind school
   too much, but I don't like leaving Leo.
   It breaks your HEART. Leo is lonely and
   missing me all day. A lot of kids don't
   like school too much. (Boring science,
   boring poetry, etc.) They need a new
   sign. WE LOVE DOGS. BRING YOUR DOG TO SCHOOL!
   Now kids love school! Teachers are
   smiling all day! The dogs of the city
   aren't lonely anymore!

3. YANKEE STADIUM. NO DOGS ALLOWED! Once
   my father took me to a baseball game.
   We had franks. Then ice-cream pops.
   Then I wanted to go home, but we had to
   watch the whole game. My father believes
   in watching the whole game even if the
   Yankees lose 11-0. Which they did. The
   fans were mad and mean and booing, and
   you felt sorry for the Yankees. They
   need a new sign.

WE LOVE DOGS. BRING YOUR DOG TO YANKEE STADIUM!
Dogs don't care if you lose a game 11-0.
They love you no matter what.

For a better New York . . . a lot of signs
that say, WE LOVE DOGS, etc.

THE END

March 29

Dear Leo,

I'm in a bad mood. Why? Because my father doesn't understand me. Plus, he never lets me do anything. It's always, *NO, ANNIE. . . . NOT NOW, ANNIE. . . . MUST WE HAVE THIS CONVERSATION AGAIN, ANNIE? YOU'RE MAKING ME LATE AND MY NIGHT STUDENTS ARE WAITING, ANNIE. . . .* blah, blah, blah. You know what I *don't* need, Leo? A *babysitter.* We *like* Mrs. Peterman (she's very, very nice), but I'm way too old for a babysitter every second of my life, and that's all there is to it.

IMPORTANT SUBJECT: STAYING HOME ALONE WITHOUT A GROWN-UP. ~~I can do it.~~

We can do it. We're *responsible.* Obviously.

1. We know about locking the door!
2. We know about no strangers in the house!
3. We're not babies!
4. We have a strong and handsome guard dog in the house! (Meaning *you*, Leo.)

GRRRRRRR

March 30

Dear Leo,

I used to like fourth-grade science, but not
anymore. It's because of Chapter 7, "Our Amazing
Human Body." I hate saying all those human body
words (hair follicles, nostrils, gallbladders, etc.) out
loud in school! Just to be sure I don't have to say
them, I don't raise my hand anymore in science.
Ever. My plan was working fine, but today it stopped
working. I didn't raise my hand as usual, but Mrs.
Meanest called on me anyway, and I had to say
"large intestine" in front of the whole class. It was
my greatest humiliation.

Your amazing human,
Annie

March 31

Dear Leo,

Jean-Marie was too long. In the girls' room. Mrs. B said, ANNIE, PLEASE FIND JEAN-MARIE. Which I did. In the girls' room. She was looking in the mirror. Brushing her hair and crying. I hate when Jean-Marie cries. Then I feel like crying, too. She told me bad news. It's about New Jersey. She's moving. To New Jersey. That's extra-bad news. She gets a big yard over there. Plus a big house. Plus her own room. No more sharing with her brother. His name is Charley, the same as my reading buddy, and they're both in first grade. It's not fair. I want to be a big sister, too, and I wouldn't even mind sharing my room. Anyway, what's SHE crying about? I'M the one who's stuck in room 245 with NO BEST FRIEND IN MY CLASS if she moves away. You NEED a best friend in your class. It's the most important thing. Now I'll have no one (in my class).

Of course, you're my *truest best friend*, Leo. You'll never move away. Ever. Ever. Ever. Not even for five minutes.

Annie

April 1

Dear Leo,

Mrs. B was in a good mood. A really good mood, and she was even *humming*. Then Tommy called out, I NEVER KNEW YOU LIKE TO SING, MRS. BAILEY. She wasn't mad that he called out. Mrs. B: WELL, I'M HAPPY TODAY. MY FAVORITE AUTHOR IS COMING TO TOWN IN A COUPLE OF WEEKS. Wow! My teacher knows an AUTHOR! I always wanted to see a live AUTHOR! I raised my hand. (Model citizens raise their hand.) She didn't call on me. I raised it some more. (Model citizens wait their turn.) She still didn't call on me. I didn't *mean* to call out, but I had a great idea. My greatest-ever idea! MAYBE THE AUTHOR COULD COME TO ROOM 245! WE COULD SEE A LIVE AUTHOR AND GET HIS AUTOGRAPH AND HE CAN TELL US ABOUT HOW TO BE AN AUTHOR!

Two things happened after that.

THING #1: I WASN'T IN TROUBLE FOR CALLING OUT!

THING #2: MRS. B LIKED MY IDEA! SHE SAID, HMMM . . . I'LL SEE WHAT THE AUTHOR HAS TO SAY ABOUT ANNIE'S GOOD IDEA.

Now I was in a good mood, too! It's about time a grown-up liked my great ideas.

Love,
Me

April 2

Dear Leo,

First he was late coming home from work, so I was
mad about that. Me: YOU'RE LATE, DADDY. Then
he forgot it was the night of the PS 88 ART FAIR, so
I was mad about that. Me: I TOLD YOU A MILLION
TIMES IT'S TONIGHT! Then he was on the phone
with that dinner party lady and I was mad about
that. Me: I HOPE YOU'RE NOT GETTING MARRIED
TO *HER*. BECAUSE IF YOU DO, I'M TAKING LEO
TO CALIFORNIA. Then we left. It was raining and I
love walking at night in the rain, so I stopped being
mad. In the rain. Then we got to school and all the
lights were on and everyone was there and all the
teachers were dressed up and they didn't look like
teachers. I kept looking and looking for my painting
in the All-Purpose Room. Me: CLOSE YOUR EYES,
DADDY. . . . NO PEEKING. . . . IT'S A SURPRISE!
Then I found it! OKAY, DADDY! OPEN YOUR EYES!

We looked at my painting for a long time and he was very, very quiet. Then he kissed the top of my head. We both looked at my painting some more.

LEO AND THE PROFESSOR, 7:30 A.M.

A Quote from the Artist: This is a picture of my dog (Leo) and my father (the Professor). Leo loves to watch my father shave. My father loves to talk to Leo when he's shaving. MORNING, LEO. SLEEP WELL, MY FRIEND? It's a painting about love.

April 5

Dear Leo,

Mrs. B caught Edward working on his Henry the goldfish comic book during math time and she took it away and said, EDWARD, I'M SURPRISED AT YOU. YOU CAN COLLECT THIS AFTER SCHOOL. I felt a little sorry for Edward.

Love,
Annie

Edward

April 9

Dear Leo,

I'm a really good and really excellent reading
buddy, but today Charley was a HUGE PAIN IN
THE NECK . . . sticking out his tongue . . . making
airplane noises . . . saying, I DON'T WANNA
READ . . . YOU CAN'T MAKE ME READ, etc.

Then I was FED UP. I said, GOOD-BYE,
CHARLEY! I'M NOT YOUR READING BUDDY
ANYMORE! Then he burst out crying. It was the
loudest noise you ever heard, and his nose was
dripping like a *leaky faucet*. I didn't want his teacher
to hear. Because his teacher was also my first-grade
teacher, Mrs. Levine. She taught me how to read
when I was a little first grader and I'm such a good
reader. What if she hears Charley crying? She'll
be *mad* at Annie Rossi and there goes my great
reputation. She'll tell her husband the principal on
me! Charley was crying, crying, crying away and I
kept saying, SORRY! I'M SORRY! I'LL ALWAYS BE
YOUR READING BUDDY! But he just kept crying.
With his head on his desk. Then I thought of one

magic word. Which is *gum*. I gave him my last piece. Well, that was the end of crying.

You probably don't know this but it's HARD being a teacher. *Exhausting*. (My father always says that about a hundred times every day and I never knew what in the world he was talking about, but now I do know.)

Your excellent reading buddy,

Annie

April 12

Dear Leo,

Does my father look lonely to you? Because elderly parents are often lonely. I read that. In that library book YOU AND YOUR ELDERLY PARENT: TIPS FOR GETTING ALONG AND HAVING FUN. Which I found again. In the library. Dr. Silvio Silverman knows a lot. We better do everything he says. Such as Tip #7.

TIP #7: ENCOURAGE YOUR ELDERLY PARENT TO KEEP UP WITH FRIENDS, BOTH OLD AND NEW. BE PREPARED FOR THE POSSIBILITY OF ROMANCE.

The Possibility of Romance...

I sure like that word *romance*! It sounds like TV, like Mrs. Peterman's soap operas on TV! Mrs. Peterman sure loves talking about *falling in love*! FRANKLY, THERE'S NOTHING LIKE IT, ANNIE. IT'S QUITE MAGICAL, THIS THING CALLED FALLING IN LOVE. Ha, ha! Ha! Never! Never! Never!

Not romantically yours,
Annie

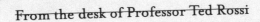

From the desk of Professor Ted Rossi

I think mostly my father looks a little lonely at night ... when he falls asleep on the couch and the lights are still on and his clothes are still on and there's always a book on his belly. He dreams about my mother, and in his dream he's not lonely anymore.

April 14

Deffinetly *(crossed out)*
Definitely

Dear Leo,

It was Pauline's turn to spell *definitely* in the spelling bee, and my turn was coming up after Jamie. Then it sounded like a big fat cow in room 245, but it was only Edward going, UGH, UGH, UGH, MY STOMACH IS KILLING ME, MRS. B. Then BAD LUCK. Mrs. B picked ME. To take Edward to the nurse and be <u>nice</u> to Creepo the Creep, who got ME in trouble in gym and who makes ME do all the work on our museum report. I didn't want Mrs. B to be mad at me, so I pretended I couldn't WAIT to take him to the nurse. I pretended

· 86 ·

who CARES about winning the spelling bee. I pretended
to have a *kind heart*. (A model citizen does a good deed
with a *kind heart*.) Me: DON'T WORRY. WE'RE ALMOST
THERE, EDWARD. . . . DON'T THROW UP HERE. . . .
NOT YET, EDWARD, etc. We finally got to the nurse.
Good-bye, good luck.

Your 100% kindly citizen,

Annie

April 15

Dear Leo,

In the morning my picture was on the bulletin board!
And a little story about my important good deed. Which
was taking poor old sick E to the nurse.

MODEL CITIZEN, ANNIE ROSSI.

But now I feel terrible. See, I'm not a *true* model
citizen. I'm a *fake*. Because my heart wasn't kind
(taking E to the nurse). I'll tell you a deep dark secret.
My heart was a little on the *mean* side. Also, I walked on
the other side of the hallway the whole time, far away
from Edward.

Your faker,
Annie

MODEL CITIZEN,
Annie Rossi

April 19

Dear Leo,

Remember that famous tug-of-war picture I took?
You and my father and his favorite green sock? And
you won the tug-of-war, remember? I showed it to
Miss Meadows after school, and Jean-Marie came,
too, and of course she was *hogging* Miss Meadows.
She kept sighing and then she told Miss Meadows
about how she's moving in four weeks to
New Jersey.

JEAN-MARIE: IF I HAD A DOG LIKE LEO,
THEN I WOULDN'T CRY FOR THE REST OF MY
LIFE IN NEW JERSEY.

MISS MEADOWS: IF YOU ASK ME, THE WORLD IS A BRIGHTER PLACE BECAUSE THERE ARE DOGS IN IT!

Don't you *love* that, Leo? Now we know
something important. *Miss Meadows
likes kids AND dogs!
I gave her the picture to keep.
I like being a nice person,
but I wish I had it back.
I really love that funny picture.

Your dearest picture taker,

April 21

Dear Leo,

You don't want to live in New Jersey, do you?
Because Jean-Marie said the same exact thing three
days in a row. Monday. Tuesday. Wednesday. DOGS
NEED FRESH AIR, ANNIE. DOGS NEED FRESH AIR,
ANNIE. THERE'S A LOT OF FRESH AIR IN NEW
JERSEY, AND LEO WOULD BE *SOOOOO* HAPPY IN
HIS BIG BACKYARD. HIS LUNGS WOULD BE HAPPY
IN NEW JERSEY.

Don't worry, baby. My father says we have a lot
of air, right here, in the city. And it's PLENTY FRESH.
He told me that.

Your city girl,

Annie

April 22

Dear Leo,

I met the Author, Harry Hope! That's Mrs. B's favorite Author and he came to room 245! Mrs. B hugged the Author, yikes! Then he sat in her chair and we sat on the floor! He's pretty old (white hair, etc.) and a little on the shy side. I never knew that an Author is a little on the shy side. He lives in faraway Maine. A long time ago he was a fourth-grader, too. Just like us. In New York City! Just like us. He told us a lot of things and nobody was calling out. We were extremely polite to the Author. Then he showed us his new book, and the pictures he made for his new book, and guess what? It's sixteen pictures and sixteen poems. I was surprised a nice man like that writes *poems*. Mrs. B asked him to read one. Harry Hope told us to close our eyes if we want; it's a nice way to get to know a poem. I never knew you get to know a poem if you close your eyes. I closed them halfway and he read to us. The poem is "Snow on a Bridge." It's about a baby in a carriage on a bridge in the snow. There's a dog, too, and a mom. It's not an *adventure* poem. All they do is go across (in the snow), but I started to cry. In front of the Author and everyone else.

   Then Mrs. B came over. LET'S GO OUTSIDE FOR A MOMENT, ANNIE. We went in the hallway, to the stairwell, and we sat on the top step. I cried some more. I felt like a big fat idiot crybaby.

Mrs. B: THAT POEM IS BEAUTIFUL, ISN'T IT?

Me: Cry, cry.

Mrs. B: DO YOU LIKE A SECRET?

Me: Cry, cry.

Mrs. B: HARRY HOPE IS *MY FATHER*.

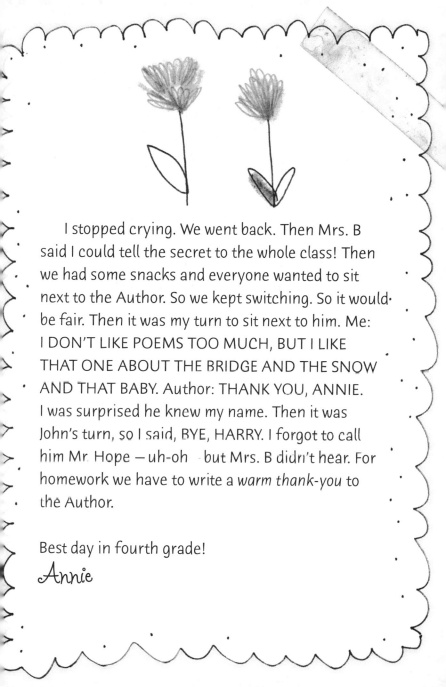

I stopped crying. We went back. Then Mrs. B said I could tell the secret to the whole class! Then we had some snacks and everyone wanted to sit next to the Author. So we kept switching. So it would be fair. Then it was my turn to sit next to him. Me: I DON'T LIKE POEMS TOO MUCH, BUT I LIKE THAT ONE ABOUT THE BRIDGE AND THE SNOW AND THAT BABY. Author: THANK YOU, ANNIE. I was surprised he knew my name. Then it was John's turn, so I said, BYE, HARRY. I forgot to call him Mr. Hope — uh-oh — but Mrs. B didn't hear. For homework we have to write a *warm thank-you* to the Author.

Best day in fourth grade!
Annie

Dear Harry Hope,

Thank you for coming to room 245 to tell us
all about your interesting life. I didn't
know Mrs. Bailey is your child! I liked
when you said you got in trouble in school.
I liked when you told us you draw a picture
FIRST and THEN you write a poem. I liked
when you said, A POEM TELLS A STORY. I
never knew that. Mrs. B forgot to tell us
that.

I will read your books and poems in
the future. I hope I like them! I like to
write stories. Also I wrote an essay for a
contest. If you come back to room 245 we
could have a party again. In June you will
be someone's grampa! Good-bye, good luck!

Your fan,
Annie Rossi

P.S. Please answer questions. It's
important. Thank you.

Are you famous?
How old are you?
Do you like being an Author?
Is it hard being an Author?
Where do you get your ideas?

P.P.S. My father is almost an Author. He
likes to write about my mother, but so far,
no book. Just scribble, scribble.

April 23

Dear Leo,

I liked the packing part best. Because packing a suitcase is fun, and choosing what to take to the sleepover. Which pajamas? Which book? Which picture of Leo? Etc. Also I liked setting up the sleeping bags in Jean-Marie's room, and mine was in the middle, between Pauline's and Jean-Marie's. I like the snacks. You have great snacks at a sleepover.

The problem is the *sleeping* part of a sleepover. Because when the lights are out, you think about your own bed and your own room and your own father and your little dog and before you know it, you're 50% sad. Then 60% . . . then 80% . . . then 100% sad.

ME: I HAVE TO GO HOME NOW.

JEAN-MARIE: YOU'RE NOT ALLOWED. YOU HAVE TO SLEEP OVER AT A SLEEPOVER.

ME: LEO MISSES ME WHEN I'M NOT THERE. HE CAN'T FALL ASLEEP IF I'M NOT HOME. HE CRIES LIKE CRAZY.

I changed my mind. The best part about the sleepover was when you and Daddy picked me up! You know what's funny? I never used to think my father was too brave, but tonight he was very brave. He went out in the dark night! At ten at night! To rescue me!

We all walked home in the dark-and-spooky night—I and you and my father. We like home, don't we, Leo? And now I am home! In my very own bed with my very own blanket and my very own moon outside my very own window. See, Leo?
See the moon?
Good night,
good night!

Your very own,
Annie

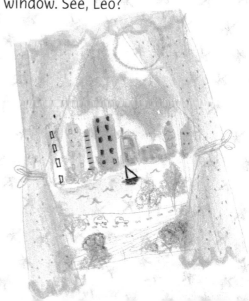

April 26

Dear Leo,

Tommy was reading his BORING report. It's about how to build a bridge, etc. It's the most BORING report you ever heard, and he's the most boring reader you ever heard. You're not supposed to doodle when someone is reading his boring report, but too bad. I doodled a girl. Ooops! She's holding someone's hand! Then I doodled her mom. I put them on a bridge. Then I wrote some words . . . and they came out a poem. I was SHOCKED and SURPRISED about how I wrote a poem. Then later on I went up to Mrs. B and said, I WROTE A POEM, MRS. B. IF YOU WANT, YOU CAN SEE IT. Then she was reading my poem for a long time, with a serious face and rubbing her tummy (big baby inside). Then she said, ANNIE, I HOPE YOU WILL SHARE THIS BEAUTIFUL AND HEARTFELT POEM WITH YOUR FATHER . . . AND OTHERS WHO ARE SPECIAL IN YOUR LIFE. I love Mrs. Bailey!

SPECIAL IN MY LIFE:

my dog
my father
Mrs. Peterman
~~Jean-Marie~~
Miss Meadows

Your Poet,
Annie

Dad (scruffy!!)

Mrs. Peterman (nice)

My Dog (Leo!)

Miss Meadows (pretty + smart)

Jean-Marie (Boo)

April 28

Dear Leo,

I showed Miss Meadows my poem that I wrote, and guess what happened? She invited me to read my poem to her class, and that's what I did! She said, BOYS AND GIRLS, WE ARE SO LUCKY TODAY. HERE IS ANNIE ROSSI, OUR VISITING POET FROM THE FOURTH GRADE! WE ARE HONORED THAT SHE WANTS TO SHARE HER POEM WITH US, AND LET'S REMEMBER OUR MANNERS!

At first I was SO scared. What if they didn't like my poem? What if my voice was too shaky? What if I sneezed LOUD in the middle of reading my poem and everyone laughed at me? Miss Meadows stood next to me when I was reading. Then it was over and everyone clapped. Even Miss Meadows. Then a girl named Ruby raised her hand. Ruby: I WISH ANNIE COULD BE IN OUR CLASS EVERY DAY.

It's my favorite day in fourth grade. Tied with my other favorite day when Harry Hope came to my class.

Your visiting Poet,

Annie

THE BROOKLYN BRIDGE
by Annie Rossi

Once,
We walked
Across
The Brooklyn Bridge
All the way to Brooklyn!
Just
The
Two of us
(I and my mother)
And
It was raining
That day

Her
Umbrella
Was big!
And yellow!
And we walked
Underneath
Very close

All the way to Brooklyn
Holding hands
And
All the way back
Holding hands

April 3

Dear Leo,

It's the second time in my life I went to a baseball game with my father. This is what I liked: The subway ride to Yankee Stadium; the ice-cream sandwiches at Yankee Stadium; and counting the stars in the sky over our heads at Yankee Stadium. Also I liked wearing matching (Yankee) baseball caps with my father. Everything else was b-o-r-i-n-g. Plus, I was freezing cold. Teeth chattering, etc. He kept giving me his ugly brown sweater to wear. Which I wasn't in the mood to wear. Plus, I couldn't find my left glove. Plus, he wouldn't let me have a second ice-cream sandwich. *I pretended to have the best time in the world. I mean it. I'm serious. I tried. But deep down I wished the Yankees would lose. Lose, lose, lose! Right this minute, so I can go home! Then I felt MEAN. Because my father LOVES his Yankees so much.

A long time later they won — Hurrah! and we *finally* came home.

Your Yankee,

Annie

me

Dad

May 3

Dear Leo,

For the first time in the history of fourth grade, science was fun, and now I like science! We are learning about EXERCISE. Everyone has to make a chart. About OUR DAILY EXERCISE. My chart is great and glorious! Even Mrs. B likes my chart. She said she might put it out for the Science Fair so everyone can see my great-and-glorious chart! She wrote: ANNIE KEEP UP THE GOOD WORK IN SCIENCE. That's the most great-and-glorious thing that ever happened in science.

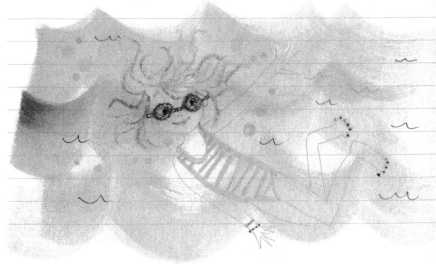

annie's MeRRY EXERCISE CHART

1. I walk to school 1 mile. (Exercise!)
2. I walk home from school 1 mile. (Exercise!)
3. I have gym 3 times a week. (Exercise!)
4. I ride a bike. (Exercise!)
5. I'm a good swimmer. (Exercise!)
6. I'm the third fastest girl runner in room 245. (Exercise!)

Mrs. B says we have to get the grown-ups in our lives to exercise. Everyone was laughing so hard when she said that. Usually we don't laugh too much in room 245, due to you have to be SERIOUS.

Your scientist,

Annie

And don't forget your exercise, Leo!

May 5

Dear Leo,

Wouldn't you know? Jean-Marie got to be model citizen today. It's only because she's moving. Also because she's perfect. She'll have a new best friend in her new class . . . and good-bye, Annie.

Love,
Me

I might write her a letter. So she doesn't forget me. Or I might get her a present. So she doesn't forget me.

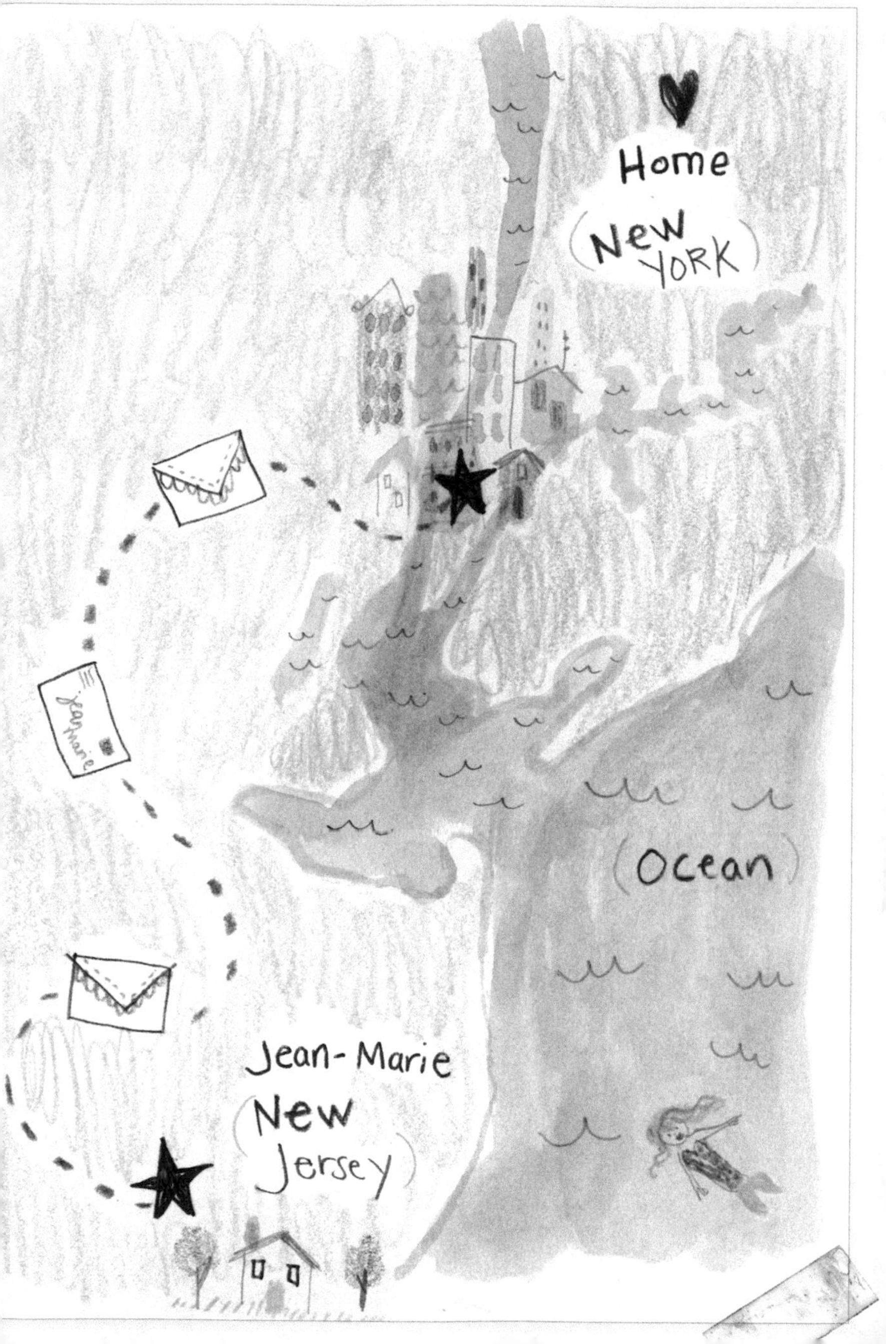

Home
(New YORK)
jean marie
(Ocean)
Jean-Marie
(New Jersey)

Miss Meadows

May 6

Dear Leo,

Your greatest spy (me) found two extremely mysterious things on Miss Meadows's desk after school.

One pair of teeny-tiny mittens, yellow!

One teeny-tiny hat, yellow!

ME: ARE YOU HAVING A <u>BABY</u>, MISS MEADOWS?

MISS MEADOWS: NO! I AM NOT!

Then she told the spy (me) an important secret. *Friday after school the teachers at my school are having a <u>surprise</u> baby-shower party for Mrs. Bailey! In the Faculty Room! The mittens and hat are presents for Mrs. B's baby!

ME: I'VE NEVER SEEN THE INSIDE OF THE FACULTY ROOM. MAYBE I COULD COME TO THE BABY-SHOWER PARTY, IF YOU WANT.

MISS MEADOWS: SORRY, ANNIE. NO KIDS ALLOWED AT THIS PARTY, OR IN THE FACULTY ROOM.

ME: KIDS MISS ALL THE GOOD STUFF.

shshhh

Then she laughed, even though it wasn't supposed to be a joke. So I laughed, too. Then I went home, good-bye.

Should greatest spy (me) tell Jean-Marie the secret? Yes. No. Yes. No.

Should greatest spy (me) tell Pauline? Yes. No. Yes. No.

Edward? Yes. No. Yes. No.

Your greatest,

Annie

May 10

Leo, Leo!

Well, I counted the days and in forty-five days guess what happens? Good-bye fourth grade! Then guess what happens? We go to the beach! You, me, my father! To our very own cottage on Pineapple Street! We have a screen door! And old bikes for the beach! And a hammock and a porch and you swim in the ocean, in the wavy, wavy ocean, if you're brave. Which I am. You know what's fun? A picnic on the beach, and there's sand in your sandwich but who cares! My mother used to run on the beach. She was fast. Like me. Like you. I wish she didn't die. I wish you could see her, Leo.

Love,
Me

YUM. YUM. YUM.

SANDWICH

PICNIC

Boooommmmmmm

May 14

Dear Leo,

ZAP!

Don't be a baby, Leo. It's just a little old thunderstorm and we are NOT afraid of thunder. Everything's fine, I promise! So cheer up, buddy! You *love* the couch and my blanket on the couch and you love being cozy. Don't worry, the NO DOGS ON THE COUCH rule doesn't count tonight. Because of the thunderstorm and because there are no grown-ups in the house. Hey! Cheer up! We *wanted* to be home alone without a grown-up, remember? One hour down and ten minutes to go . . . ten little minutes, and then my father is home!

ZAP!

CRASH HHH HH HHHHH H H H

ZAP!

Okay, I've got my eye on the front door . . . and NO ONE comes through that door . . . only my father . . . in nine minutes. I know what you're thinking. You're thinking there's a ROBBER out there on the other side of the door. But don't worry, Leo, robbers <u>never</u> come out on a stormy night. They don't have raincoats. It's true. I mean it. I'm serious.

Okay, I am now going to tell you something important, but you can't tell a soul. Ready? I HATE being home alone without a grown-up . . . and we are NEVER doing this again for as long as we both shall live.

May 17

Dear Leo,

Edward was taking too long getting to art so Mrs. Pasternak said, ANNIE, PLEASE TRACK DOWN YOUR CLASSMATE EDWARD. I tracked him down. In the stairwell, and you never saw a sadder sight than the sight of Edward Noble in the stairwell today. I know why. He told me why. It's about Henry, the noble goldfish. He died. Now two of us were sad in the stairwell. Then we went to art. Edward wouldn't do art. He just kept looking down on his lap, in that teeny little comic book, the one he made about Henry. I didn't tell on E. I'm not that kind of person.

Your kindest,
Annie

May 19

Dear Leo,

Wasn't it crazy! When we saw Miss Meadows in the park! I never knew she goes to Riverside Park like we do! At first I was a little shy — and my father was a little shy, too. (He is not a social butterfly.) I like when Miss Meadows said, AND <u>YOU</u> MUST BE LEO, and then you did a lot of showing off and wagging. You weren't shy, Leo! My favorite thing was her orange sweatshirt. I never knew she has an orange sweatshirt! My second favorite thing was how she told you a secret in your ear. I wish she told me a secret, too. Then she said good-bye and then she was gone. Then my father said those two interesting things. Remember, Leo?

Miss Meadows

WHAT MY FATHER SAID:

 LEO CERTAINLY LIKES MISS MEADOWS.

 MISS MEADOWS IS QUITE FRIENDLY.

Hmmm. Interesting.

Love,
Me

All my life, my whole entire life, my favorite color is red.
Except for a month or so when I was six when it was
purple. But I might change to orange. I like orange. And
also Miss Meadows.

May 21

Okay, Leo, I shall now read something interesting. To you. It's my report for the Science fair.

I ♥ my Bicycle.

Science Fair Report
by Annie Rossi, fourth grade

Getting My Father to Ride a Bike

Hi. My name is Annie Rossi, and it's important to get the grown-ups in our lives to EXERCISE. I love to ride my bike and I love my father. But HE doesn't love to ride a bike anymore. A quote from my father: I SEEM TO HAVE LOST MY OLD BICYCLE CONFIDENCE, ANNIE. It's a big shame because *I* have a lot of fun, but *he* doesn't have too much fun. Plenty of elderlies ride a bike. I have seen them in the park. They aren't fast like me on a bike, but that's okay. Being a slowpoke is not a criminal act, ha, ha! I have a good idea about getting the grown-up in my life to ride a bike. My father is always serious so I will have a serious talk with him. This is what I will say, DADDY, YOU HAVE TO RIDE A BIKE. IT'S FUN, PLUS GOOD FOR YOUR BONES AND LUNGS AND LEGS. IT'S <u>EXERCISE.</u>

THE END

And here's what Mrs. Bailey wrote on the other side of my report:

Annie,
This is a very enthusiastic report. Excellent! See? Didn't I tell you? Science isn't so bad. Good luck getting your father to exercise. Given that you are such a talented bike rider yourself, how about giving him a lesson? It will surely boost his confidence. Sometimes even a grown-up needs a good boost!
Mrs. B

I made up my mind. I shall be my father's teacher! I shall give him a bicycle lesson. Wish me good luck! I need it! Ha, ha!

ONE COUPON
for
Professor Ted Rossi

AND YOU WILL RECEIVE ONE BICYCLE LESSON!
FREE OF CHARGE! YO HO HO! YOUR TEACHER'S NAME?
ANNIE. ANNIE ROSSI.

WHEN: SATURDAY, 11:00 A.M.
WHERE: RIVERSIDE PARK
WHAT TO WEAR: <u>FUN</u> CLOTHES, NOT YOUR
USUAL TEACHER CLOTHES
WHAT TO BRING: YOUR OLD BIKE THAT YOU
NEVER RIDE ANYMORE

COME ON Mr.
S-L-O-W-P-O-K-E
!!!!!! FASTER,
FASTER, TURN ON
THE SPEEEEE
EEEEED!
(oh, no.)

May 22

Dear Leo,

What a giant catastrophe. The whole terrible thing, and it's all my fault and I'm definitely the most horrible teacher in the world. And the most horrible child in the world. And the stupidest show-off in the world. I *never* show off. I'm not that kind of girl, but today I was showing off. Going fast on the hill and telling my father to be fast like me. COME ON, MR. SLOWPOKE! TURN ON THE SPEED!

Then he was flying over his handlebars. Which was a terrible thing to watch. Obviously. Plus, he disappeared. In the bushes. Super-terrible.

Now his finger is *so* black *and* blue *and green* and *fat*. Poor, poor Daddy. Stuck with me for a child. Everything I do is terrible. I shall never say the word *exercise* again.

Your most horrid,

Annie

Thank you for being a perfect little angel dog tonight. I noticed you've been keeping an eye on my father all night long. He sits down. Then you sit down. He gets up. Then you get up. He goes to the kitchen. Then you go to the kitchen. I like what he said about you. It's very beautiful. Like a poem! I NEVER KNEW I WOULD LIKE A DOG. BUT THIS FELLOW? I MUST SAY, THIS FELLOW IS GROWING ON ME.

He loves you, Leo. And so do I.

Annie

May 26

Dear Leo,

Well, of COURSE you're not supposed to read other people's mail, but too bad. I was *painfully* curious when mysterious flowers arrived for my father. *Who is sending flowers to my father?* Mrs. Peterman was curious, too. There was a card inside an envelope. The envelope was sealed, boooo! My father was at work! We couldn't wait, we *had* to peek. Sorry.

Professor Rossi,

Annie told me about your tumble in the park, your little flight to nowhere. Well, take care of yourself . . . and about that bike, don't give up!

Warm regards,
Maggie Meadows

Mrs. Peterman liked the note. You could tell she liked the note because she was smiling and nodding and her eyebrows went up.

Then he came home. He laughed when he saw the flowers. He laughed when he read the card. Mrs. Peterman gave me a look that means YOUR FATHER DOESN'T USUALLY LAUGH TWO TIMES IN A ROW, ANNIE.

I want Miss Meadows to come over. Here. To our house. I could show her my room. And if it's night we look out the windows at the moon, and stars, and boats on the Hudson River. Then we go sneaking inside and we spy on my father awhile. And I tell her some interesting secrets. About my father. Such as he's really, really nice. And he's good at lots of things. Such as reading. Writing. Teaching the college kids. And hamburgers. And grilled-cheese sandwiches. And if you can't sleep, he stays up with you — even if it's midnight — until you finally fall asleep. *I tell how he never used to like and love dogs, but now Leo is his friend, and that's the very best thing I tell Miss Meadows!

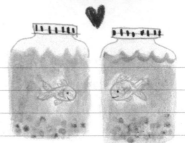

June 5

Dear Leo,

A good friend shares. I'm not a good friend. Which I told my father. Last night. When we were walking you. When I couldn't fall asleep.

ME: I MIGHT SEND LEO TO NEW JERSEY FOR A WHILE. SO JEAN-MARIE ISN'T TOO LONELY.

MY FATHER: HAVE YOU DISCUSSED THIS WITH LEO?

ME: HE DOESN'T WANT TO GO.

MY FATHER: GOOD. BECAUSE HE'S AN IMPORTANT MEMBER OF THE ROSSI FAMILY. THIS FAMILY WOULDN'T BE THE SAME WITHOUT LEO.

ME: A MODEL CITIZEN *SHARES*. A GOOD FRIEND *SHARES*.

MY FATHER: PERHAPS. BUT GIVING AWAY YOUR DOG IS *NOT* A REQUIREMENT FOR EITHER CATEGORY. ANYWAY, YOU'RE MORE THAN A GOOD FRIEND, IN MY OPINION, AND

MORE THAN A MODEL CITIZEN. YOU'RE THE BEST DAUGHTER IN THE WORLD.
 ME: AND YOU'RE THE BEST FATHER. IN THE WORLD.

Then today, for the first time in the history of my life, my father has a great idea! It has to do with goldfish. And we went to the pet shop on Broadway and picked out one skinny goldfish – a present for Jean-Marie! And one chubby goldfish – a present for Edward!

I carried them home in two plastic bags, and we took two old mayonnaise jars and filled them with water and colorful pebbles at the bottom. It looked like two goldfish in two houses. They swam around, and sometimes they looked at each other. Me: THEY'RE FALLING IN LOVE. My father: IS THAT SO? Me: IT'S QUITE MAGICAL, REALLY. MRS. PETERMAN TOLD ME. SHE KNOWS A LOT. ABOUT FALLING IN LOVE. IT'S BECAUSE OF THOSE SOAP OPERAS. ON TV.

Remember to *share*, Leo.

Annie

June 12

Dear Leo,

Ten more days of school, tra laaa! Ten more days of
school, tra laaa! Summertime, tra laaa! We're going to
the beach! To our cottage at the beach! We'll fool around
all day! Every single day! In the ocean, on the beach, on
the hammock, on the porch! We walk to town! And take
my bike to town! Meet me at the beach! No shoes at the
beach! All summer long!

Your summer girl,

Annie

One more thing. My father got you a special dog tag.
Purple! It means you have permission to come on the
train, Leo. All the way to 45 Pineapple Street. You
have to be good. Absolutely NO funny stuff on the
train. Or the conductor will be mad at my father, and
that's terrible. So just be a model dog, okay? We always
have a picnic on the train. It's a Rossi family tradition.

Meaning egg-salad sandwiches and chocolate milk in a thermos. You look out the window a lot. The train stops eight times and then you're at the beach!

Train Stops

#1
#2
#3
#4
#5
#6
#7
#8

45 PINEAPPLE ST.

June 14

Dear Leo,

We had a sub and no Mrs. Bailey. Then Mr. Levine came in. GOOD MORNING, BOYS AND GIRLS. I RECEIVED AN INTERESTING CALL AT SIX THIS MORNING. <u>STANLEY</u> BAILEY HAS ARRIVED, WEIGHING IN AT A HEALTHY SIX POUNDS. MOTHER, FATHER, AND STANLEY ARE ALL DOING FINE. CONGRATULATIONS TO MRS. BAILEY'S CLASS.

It was so, so quiet. Then he left. Still so quiet. Then it wasn't quiet anymore. We all got crazy! Screaming and jumping and dancing around the room! I forgot to be mad it's not a girl. I forgot her name isn't Annie.

Then the sub forgot we have art after gym on Monday.

Then the sub forgot to give us a math test.

Then the sub forgot to give us homework.

It was a pretty good day in fourth grade. Obviously!

Annie

June 16

Dear Leo,

The best part about *not* winning was when we went to
the park to cheer me up. Then my father said, WELL,
LOOK AT THIS, LEO! A COPY OF ANNIE'S ESSAY! THE
GREAT ONE WITH HER GREAT IDEAS FOR A BETTER
NEW YORK! RIGHT HERE IN MY POCKET! Then we sat
on a bench and he read it out loud and we snuggled up
close. You on one side of him and me on the other.

  Then we went home and picked up the mail and
there was a letter for me! From HIS HONOR, THE
MAYOR OF NEW YORK CITY! I'm keeping it for the rest
of my life!

Dear Annie,

I really enjoyed your inspiring essay.
Thank you for sharing those beautiful
ideas for a better New York. I am pleased
to award you this *Certificate For Writing
Excellence* and wish you good luck in the
future.

Yours sincerely,
His Honor, the Mayor of the City
of New York

The certificate is so beautiful, and I'm putting it on the table next to my bed. Next to that picture of my mother.

Love,

Me

P.S. I still wish Annie Rossi won the contest first place, not Melvin in room 207. A boy, of all things. A fifth-grade boy.

INTERESTING SUBJECT: MISS MEADOWS.

I told her about my certificate. Me: I MIGHT PUT IT IN A FRAME. ORANGE! Miss Meadows: MAYBE YOU CAN SHOW ME YOUR ESSAY SOMETIME. IF YOU'RE IN THE MOOD. Then I didn't want to talk about my essay anymore. Me: DO YOU HAVE SOME FRIENDS? Miss Meadows: YES, ANNIE, I DO. BUT I'M *ALWAYS* LOOKING FOR NEW ONES.
Me: MY FATHER SAYS YOU'RE *QUITE FRIENDLY*. IF YOU WANT, YOU COULD BE *HIS* FRIEND. IF YOU WANT.

You know what's a little sad? When you look at Jean-Marie's empty seat, due to she's in another seat, Leo. Far away in New Jersey. But guess what! Mrs. Bailey is coming to school with Stanley! Tomorrow! So Stanley can see us! I want to hold him. And guess what else! Harry Hope sent our class a picture that he made, and he's writing a poem to go with the picture! It's going to be about Stanley!

I wrote a poem, too, and I'm giving it to Mrs. B. For a present. Aren't I charming, ha! Her name is in my poem. And yours is, too.

The Dog Did It
A Quite Charming Poem, by Annie Rossi, Room 245

The
Dog
Ate my homework
And I'm
Sorry
Mrs. Bailey
Very *sorry*
Mrs. Bailey

I am
Shocked
Annie Rossi
Quite *shocked*
Annie Rossi
Now, off to the principal you go

The
Dog
Ate my homework
And
I LOVE HIM
Mrs. Bailey
Leo! Leo!
I LOVE YOU!

June 25

Dear Leo,

I shall now sing to you. Ready?

Farewell, Fourth Grade!
An Inspiring Song, by Annie Rossi

Good-bye, school!
Good-bye, school!
Good-bye, school!
We love to say good-bye!

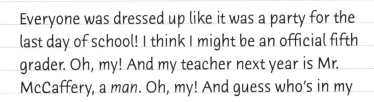

Farewell, fourth grade!
Hello, summer!
Hello, va-ca-tion!
Farewell, good-bye!

Everyone was dressed up like it was a party for the last day of school! I think I might be an official fifth grader. Oh, my! And my teacher next year is Mr. McCaffery, a *man*. Oh, my! And guess who's in my class (again) next year? The Great-and-Annoying **Edward**. Remember the goldfish that I gave Edward (due to I'm such a nice human)? Well, he *still* didn't figure out a name. So I said, ANNIE'S A GOOD NAME. But of course no one ever likes my good ideas. Not even Edward. Then after school I was waving good-bye to Miss Meadows, and Edward was in my way as usual. He said, I THOUGHT UP A NAME FOR MY GOLDFISH: Stanley, Jr.

Oh, brother.

Love from your new fifth grader,

Annie

Hang
on
Tight,
Leo!!

(Mom's old bike)

July 19

Dear Leo,

See? I TOLD you! I TOLD you you'd love our little cottage on Pineapple Street. And the beach. And the ocean. And walking to town. And watching my father wobble around on his old beach bike. AND WATCHING ME GO FAST ON MY MOTHER'S OLD GREEN BIKE that is the BEST bike in the world. See? I TOLD you being a Rossi in summertime is great!

Okay, now you have to get ready. Well, my father is finally ALMOST ready (I hope) . . . but he forgot the flower, the pretty orange flower . . . and we can't be late. Off, Leo! Off that hammock, Mr. Lazybones Leo! Someone's coming! On the 10:05, and I know you can't wait! When we get to the station, you have to be *brilliant,* in every way, the way we practiced. Stay away from those tracks, you hear? Just sit on the bench, with me on one side of you and my father on the other side of you. Can you remember that, Leo? And then it will finally be 10:05! And the train from the city will finally come clanking into the station! Then she'll get off the train. And you may *not* jump on Miss Meadows. No matter how happy you are to see her, no jumping. Can you remember that, Leo? Because she's our *guest* for the day and the rule is NO JUMPING ON THE GUESTS! Just behave yourself. I know your stomach is in knots. Well, mine is, too, and we both can't wait. Oh well, just do what I say and we all live happily ever after.

I bet she wears a hat. A big beach hat.

Love you, Leo!

Annie

By the way and in case you were wondering, I know about the possibility of romance. I watch TV.

Ta-daaa!!

(Our sand castle)

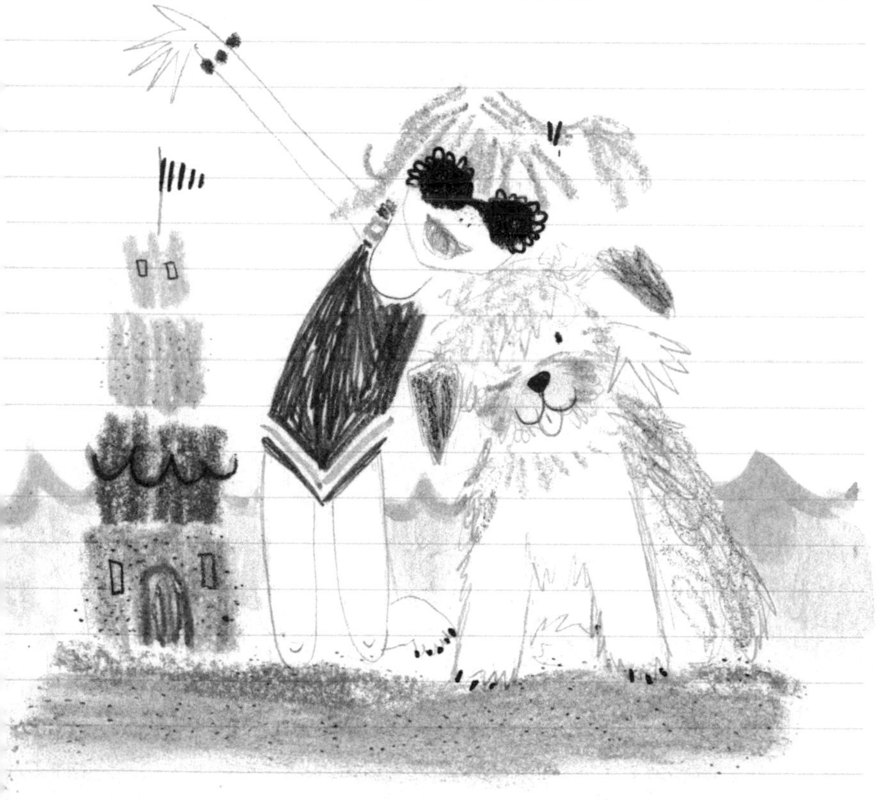